# Table of Contents

Dedicated to you. May you always find a reason to smile!

The Forgotten Carnival
A Retro Horrors: The Lost Decade Book
By: B. Humphrey

# Chapter 1:

The sun hung low on the horizon, dipping the sky into oranges and pinks that smeared across the sleepy little town. Jake Foster leaned against the hood of Riley's rusted-out Camaro, sipping a cherry Slurpee through a flimsy plastic straw. The 7-Eleven parking lot buzzed with the lazy hum of summer. BMX tires skidded against pavement, a radio crackled with Def Leppard's "Pour Some Sugar on Me," and the smell of gasoline and hot asphalt mixed with the sweetness of melting popsicles.

Jake flicked the last bits of a crumpled Marlboro pack between his fingers, wearing his usual denim jacket. It was a battle-worn relic, tattered at the cuffs and heavy with metal band patches: **Slayer, Metallica, Anthrax, Megadeth, Iron Maiden.** His mullet glinted majestically in the dying light as Riley tossed an empty soda can at him from the driver's seat.

"You gonna stand there lookin' cool, or we headin' to the arcade?" Riley grinned, drumming his fingers on the wheel. His blonde hair stuck up in all directions, looking like he'd just rolled out of bed, probably because he had.

Amber Sullivan hopped up onto the hood next to Jake, her big hoop earrings clinking lightly as she shoved a handful of **Dip 'n Dots** into her mouth.

"Pixel Palace'll be packed tonight. Everyone's gonna be there."

Her teased hair gave her another inch of height, and the light from the streetlamps made her eyeliner shimmer in the dusk.

Derrick "Dare" Nelson skidded to a halt on his BMX bike, almost toppling over as he leaned on the handlebars. His face was slick with sweat from doing tricks in the heat.

"Screw the arcade. Let's do somethin' dangerous." He flashed that familiar reckless grin, the one that usually led to trouble.

"Jump the tracks at the train yard?"

Jake shook his head, glancing down the street, where the edges of the town blurred into cornfields and woods.

"Nah," he muttered. "Not feelin' it tonight."

Amber rolled her eyes. "C'mon, Jake. You've been a downer since your sister's recital or whatever. Cheer up. It's summer dude pants."

Jake opened his mouth to argue when Dare pointed toward the edge of town. "Yo, check it out."

Everyone turned. Across the fields, bright neon lights flickered to life. Pinks, blues, and greens swirled like a kaleidoscope under the encroaching twilight.

"That wasn't there this morning," Amber whispered.

Jake squinted. "What the hell?"

A carnival. Big as a county fair, loomed just outside town, its Ferris wheel spinning slowly, silhouetted against the purple horizon. Calliope music drifted faintly on the breeze, eerie and cheerful all at once, like the kind of tune you'd hear in a dream right before it turned into a nightmare.

"That's impossible," Riley muttered, leaning forward on the wheel. "I was out there earlier, just ridin' around. There was nothin'."

"Looks like something now," Dare said, already hopping off his bike. "Let's check it out."

Jake felt uneasy, like the ground beneath him shifted slightly, just enough to make him question if he'd almost fell backwards. But then Jimmy Ortega pedaled by on his ten-speed, his face twisted with frustration.

"You guys goin' or what?" Jimmy shot a glare at Jake, his dark eyes burning with something close to betrayal.

"I'm done waitin' around. You said we'd hang out, Jake. Guess that was a lie too."

Before Jake could respond, Jimmy pushed his bike harder, tearing off toward the glowing carnival in the distance. Amber muttered under her breath, "Yikes. What's his deal?"

Jake clenched his jaw, guilt gnawing at the edges of his thoughts.

"We should go after him." Riley groaned. "Man, Jimmy's just bein' a little drama que-."

"No," Jake cut him off, already tossing his Slurpee cup into the trash. "He's pissed, and it's my fault. Let's just go get him."

The group cut through the narrow streets and onto the dirt path leading out of town, their sneakers kicking up dust in the warm night air. As they neared the carnival, the music grew louder, tinny notes that seemed to spiral on themselves, twisting and turning in unsettling ways.

The air smelled like fried dough, sugar, popcorn, and old wood, but beneath it all lingered something sour, like metal left out in the rain.

The entrance gate stood tall, a neon-lit arch buzzing with flickering carnival lights. Beneath it, a mechanical puppet in faded ringmaster attire sat slumped inside a glass booth. Its eyes dull and eerily human, seemed to follow them as they approached.

Dare reached the booth first and tapped on the glass. "Hey, creepy doll dude, gimme a ticket."

With a slow, jerking motion, the puppet straightened. The sound of gears grinding filled the air as it tilted its head toward Dare, then produced four tickets from its vest. Each one was personalized.

Jake's had a little guitar on it, Riley's a jester, Amber's a red balloon, and Dare's showed a spinning wheel. No one noticed at first, but Jimmy and his ticket was missing.

Jake's stomach churned. Something about the puppet's glassy eyes unsettled him, but before he could say anything, Dare grabbed his ticket. "Weird," he muttered, pocketing it.

Amber shivered. "This place gives me the creeps already."

Jake agreed but said nothing, following the others through the gate.

The carnival unfolded before them like a fever dream. Bright lights flashed in hypnotic patterns, and every booth seemed to hum with strange energy. Games lined the midway, their prizes swaying gently in the breeze, stuffed animals with stitched grins and wide, unblinking eyes.

A rollercoaster rumbled overhead, its cars screeching as they curved through impossible loops. A clown juggled knives by the cotton candy stand, and no one seemed to notice when one of the blades missed, embedding itself in the wooden planks.

Amber stared wide-eyed at a booth advertising "**Fortunes Told. Madame Vespera Awaits.**"

Riley nudged her with an elbow. "Looks like your kinda thing."

"LoOkS LiKe YoUr KiNdA Bleh," Amber shot back in a mocking tone, but there was nervousness in her voice.

Dare grinned. "Bet it's one of those stupid tents with a fake crystal ball. C'mon, let's get in line."

But Jake wasn't listening. He thought he saw Jimmy, just a flicker, reflected in the glass of a nearby booth. Jake stepped closer, squinting, but the reflection vanished before he could be sure. He pressed his hand to the glass, but it felt ice-cold, colder than the humid night air around them.

"Jimmy?" Jake whispered. No response. The glass remained empty except for Jake's distorted reflection, his jacket, his patches, and the unease etched across his face.

Amber tugged on his sleeve. "You good?"

"Yeah," Jake muttered. "Yeah, I'm fine, we should find Jimmy."

But he wasn't fine. Not at all. They hadn't been inside long when the carnival seemed to swallow them up.

Amber glanced at the clown tent in the distance, her skin crawling. "Imma check over there," she said reluctantly.

Jake shook his head. "We should stick together."

"We'll cover more ground if we split up," Dare argued. "Besides, we all have these weird tickets, right? Maybe we gotta follow them."

Reluctantly, Jake nodded. "Fine. But if anyone finds Jimmy, yell."

Amber gave a mock salute before heading toward the clowns, and Dare wandered off toward the carousel.

Riley clapped Jake on the back. "Guess it's you and me, huh?"

Jake forced a grin. "I recon so yo. Let's go."

As they moved deeper into the carnival, the laughter and music faded into something eerie. As if the carnival was listening, waiting. Jake clenched his ticket tightly, feeling the weight of his mistake in every step.

# Chapter 2:

The lights flickered overhead like they were alive, pulsating to the rhythm of the haunting calliope music. The midway stretched endlessly in both directions, a maze of glowing booths and swirling rides. The smell of caramel apples and popcorn coated the humid air, but beneath it was something rancid, like decaying leaves at the bottom of a swamp at low tide.

Jake and Riley walked side by side, weaving through the sea of strangers, most of whom wore vacant expressions. The visitors moved with an unnatural calm, as if drawn by some invisible force, their faces slack and eyes glazed over. Jake tightened his grip on his ticket, his knuckles whitening.

"This place ain't right," Riley muttered under his breath, kicking a stray popcorn bucket across the midway. "Feels freakin weird man."

Jake didn't respond, his gaze flickering from booth to booth. Everywhere they turned, the carnival seemed to shift, rides towering higher, paths twisting in on themselves like a dream that couldn't be mapped. Jake glanced back over his shoulder. The entrance gate was gone, swallowed by the carnival's strange geometry.

"This way," Jake said, though he wasn't sure how he knew. Something about the lights ahead, a dull, pulsing glow drew him in like the undertow of a rip current.

They came upon a tent draped in deep purple fabric, glowing softly beneath the carnival lights. A sign swung lazily above the entrance: **"Madame Vespera Awaits."**

Jake and Riley exchanged uneasy glances, but before they could back away, the tent's entrance fluttered open, as if beckoning them inside. "Guess we're goin' in this time," Riley muttered, his sarcasm barely masking the tension in his voice.

Inside, the air was thick with incense, sharp and floral, the kind that sticks to your clothes and lingers in your nose long after you leave.

Flickering lanterns cast jittery shadows on the walls, making everything seem alive. The fortune-teller sat at a small table in the center of the tent. She wore a flowing black dress, her fingers adorned with silver rings that clinked as she shuffled a deck of Dark Star tarot cards.

Her eyes glinted unnaturally in the low light, wide, glassy, and unblinking. When she smiled, her lips stretched a bit too far, as if they weren't quite used to the shape.

"You've found your way to me at last," she purred, her voice like velvet sliding around their ears, slipping in and out like some strange massage.

"Would you like to know your fortune?"

Jake stiffened. "We're just looking for someone. A kid. Jimmy Ortega. Have you seen him?"

Madame Vespera tilted her head, her smile never wavering. "Ah, but we are all searching for something, are we not?"

She flipped a card from the deck and laid it flat on the table. **The Tower.**

Riley let out a nervous laugh. "That's... not good, right?"

Madame Vespera's grin widened. "Change is inevitable my dear little one. You will find what you seek, but the price will be high."

Before Jake could ask more, the tent began to shift. The walls rippled, and the shadows stretched toward them like reaching hands.

"You'd best move along," Vespera whispered, her voice fading as if carried off by the wind. "Your friend waits on the other side of your fears."

And with that, the floor beneath them tilted, sending Jake and Riley stumbling back out into the midway. The moment they stepped outside, the carnival seemed different, quieter, more menacing. The midway stretched longer, the lights dimmer, as if the carnival was holding its breath.

Amber appeared suddenly, running toward them from the direction of the clown tent, her face pale and frantic.

"Dude, I think I saw Jimmy, just for a second, but as soon as I called him he disappeared."

"What do you mean, Disappeared?" Riley asked.

Amber looking confused responded, "Like, he just kind of faded into mist and was gone."

Jake felt a surge of cold dread wash over him. "Where?"

Amber shook her head, glancing nervously over her shoulder.

"Near the Ferris wheel, I think, but... something's wrong. It's like, like he wasn't right. It felt really bad, like I saw something I wasn't supposed to."

"Okay," Jake said, taking a steadying breath.

"Amber, you check the Ferris wheel where you saw him. Riley and I will keep looking around here and work our way around to see if we see him on the other side. And keep your tickets on you. I feel like we might need them before this is over."

Dare caught up with them, wiping sweat from his brow. "I found this weird carousel. Thought it might lead somewhere, but... it didn't feel right. It felt like it was about to, I don't know, hit me, or grab me. It felt like I needed to brace myself or run."

He looked at the others, his usual cocky grin gone. "This place... it's messin' with me man."

Jake clapped Dare on the back. "Not just you bro, this place feels really screwed up."

Riley pointed to the crowds slowly walking

Like zombies, "I mean look at them, none of them look up, or at each other, or at us. It's like they're just empty shells."

"Yeah man, Let's find Jimmy and bounce," Jake said.

With that, the group reluctantly split, each heading deeper into the carnival's tangled heart. As Jake wandered toward the towering Ferris wheel, the air grew heavier, the music distorting into off-key warbles. The wheel loomed above him, its rusted spokes groaning with every rotation. Jake's heart pounded as he spotted something flicker in the corner of his vision, Jimmy.

The boy stood at the base of the Ferris wheel, his face pale and drawn, but when Jake called his name, Jimmy turned and walked away, disappearing into the shadows.

"Jimmy, hold up dude!" Jake shouted, sprinting after him. But when he rounded the corner, there was nothing, just the skeletal outline of the Ferris wheel and the faint echoes of carnival music.

Breathless, Jake leaned against a wooden post. Something wasn't right. The air smelled faintly metallic, like blood or old pennies, and the ground beneath him felt soft, like the earth had been disturbed recently.

He glanced up at the Ferris wheel again. Its lights flickered erratically, and for a brief moment, he saw a vision of his sister, standing at the top of the wheel, calling out to him.

"Jake!" she cried, her voice small and distant. "You promised you'd be there!"

Jake's stomach churned as the vision faded.

Meanwhile, Riley stumbled across the **Tunnel of Dreams**, a narrow canal winding through a dark, artificial cavern. Boats bobbed gently along the water, their lanterns flickering like fireflies. A sign above the entrance read, **"Face Your Wildest Desires... Or Your Greatest Regrets."**

Riley hesitated, but something about the water and how it shimmered like glass drew him in. He stepped into one of the boats, which drifted forward as if it had been waiting just for him.

The tunnel walls closed in, and the air grew thick with the scent of roses and something sickly sweet, like spoiled fruit. Shadows danced along the water's surface, forming familiar shapes, his parents, arguing in the kitchen, his dad looking disappointed, his friends always making plans without him, his own reflection, twisted and sneering.

"You can't control anything," the reflection whispered, grinning back at him. "Not your friends. Not your life. Not even yourself. You can't do anything right."

Riley closed his eyes, trying to steady his breathing. The boat drifted further into the tunnel, the walls pressing closer. Visions of futures he never wanted swirled before his eyes, him, alone, forgotten, drowning in a sea of his own failures.

When the boat finally reached the end of the tunnel, **Madame Vespera was waiting.**

"Did you enjoy the ride?" she asked, her glassy eyes glinting.

Riley stared at her, his heart pounding. "What do you want from us?"

Vespera smiled, her lips curling with eerie satisfaction. "What do you want from yourself?"

Before Riley could respond, the boat was pushed back into the tunnel, the current pulling him toward the midway.

As the group reconvened near the center of the carnival, the air grew heavier with tension. The lights flickered erratically, and the ground seemed to shift beneath their feet.

"We need to find Jimmy fast," Jake said, his voice tight. "This place ain't natural bro."

Amber nodded, her face pale.

Dare kicked at the dirt, his jaw clenched, not saying a word. Jake glanced at the swirling lights overhead, the music twisting into an off-key dirge. The carnival felt alive, and hungry.

# Chapter 3:

The **Hall of Mirrors** towered before Jake and Amber, shimmering with countless reflections that stretched into the darkness. Its curved walls gleamed under the dim carnival lights, promising wonder, confusion, and something far more sinister. The entrance yawned open like a mouth, swallowing the two teens as they stepped inside.

The music outside faded into a distant hum, and the air grew heavy with stillness. The smell of dust and old glass hung thick, mixed with a faint metallic tang, like pennies in water.

Amber shivered, though the night was warm, and tucked a loose strand of hair behind her ear.

"I don't like this place," she whispered, her voice barely more than a breath. Her reflection whispered the same thing back, but the movement in the glass seemed just a bit too slow.

Jake nodded, keeping his eyes on the twisting maze ahead. The walls curved in impossible ways, mirrors reflecting mirrors until it felt like the room stretched forever.

The glass around them shimmered, their reflections multiplying, distorting into grotesque versions of themselves. Jake tried to shake off the unease, but every reflection seemed to be watching, mocking him with the smallest curl of a lip, the slightest glint of a knowing eye.

Amber glanced at one of her reflections and froze, it was smiling back, its grin stretching far too wide, splitting open at the seams like a cracked porcelain doll.

"Jake..." she whispered, her breath catching. "I don't think we're alone."

Jake turned and saw himself, standing just beyond the first mirror, but it wasn't him at all.

The reflection wore his denim jacket and patches, but the eyes were hollow empty black holes. The smile that curved across its face was sharp and menacing.

The reflection stepped closer, pressing its hands against the glass as if it might slip through at any moment. Jake took a step back, his heart pounding in his chest. "We need to move. Now."

They turned corner after corner, but every step led them deeper into the maze of mirrors. The reflections multiplying until they no longer knew where they had started. Each mirror showed a different version of them, twisted, corrupted, and wrong.

In one, Jake saw himself standing over his little sister, his face cold and emotionless, while she cried quietly in the background. In another, his sister turned away from him, her face blank with indifference, as if she had already forgotten who he was.

Jake clenched his fists, trying to focus. "This isn't real," he whispered to himself, but the doubt was already creeping in.

Amber gasped from behind him. He turned to see her reflection morphing into a grotesque clown, its face painted with jagged lines and smeared colors. The clown's eyes rolled back in its head, and its grin stretched so wide it began to split open with a wet, tearing sound.

Amber stumbled back, clutching her head. "No—no, it's not real!" she whispered, as if saying it out loud might make it true. But the clown behind the glass pressed its hands against the mirror, smearing the surface with streaks of red greasy paint. Then, slowly, deliberately, it turned its gaze toward Jake and grinned.

Jake grabbed Amber's arm, pulling her away. "We have to keep going," he urged. "It's just trying to mess with us."

Amber nodded, but her breath was shallow, and her hand trembled in Jake's grip. They pressed on, turning corner after corner, but the maze only seemed to twist tighter around them. Their footsteps echoed endlessly, as if they were walking in circles, forever trapped in a reflection of a reflection.

Just as Jake was about to suggest turning back, he saw something flicker in the corner of his vision, a shadow, a movement beyond the glass. He turned toward it, his heart hammering.

And there he was. Jimmy.

Jimmy stood behind one of the mirrors, his hands pressed against the glass. His face was pale and desperate, his dark eyes wide with fear.

"Jake, Amber, Help me please. I don't know where I am. I don't feel right Jake. I feel hollow."

Jimmy's voice was muffled, but his panic cut through the thick silence.

"Jimmy!" Jake rushed toward the mirror, placing his hands over Jimmy's. The glass was cold.

"We've got you! We'll get you out!"

Amber knelt beside Jake, pressing her hands against the mirror too.

"We're here, Jimmy! Hang on!"

But as they tried to pull him through, the reflection behind Jimmy shifted.

A hand, long and thin, with fingers that stretched unnaturally far, reached out from the darkness, wrapping around Jimmy's shoulder.

Jimmy's face twisted with terror as the hand yanked him back, pulling him deeper into the shadows.

"NO!" Jake shouted, slamming his fists against the glass. But it was too late. Jimmy was dragged back into the darkness, his scream swallowed by the mirror.

Amber gasped, her hands still pressed against the cold surface.

"What the hell is this place?"

Jake stared at the empty glass, his breath shallow and uneven.

"I don't know, but we can't leave without him," he whispered.

As they tried to find a way deeper into the maze, the mirrors around them began to shift and twist.

Their reflections no longer mirrored their movements. Instead, they moved on their own, whispering things to each other, laughing, and at times it felt like they were mocking them.

Amber's hands trembled, her fear building until it bubbled over. With a sharp cry, she slammed her fist into the nearest mirror.

"Stop it!" She screamed.

The glass shattered with a deafening crack, shards flying in every direction. For a moment, everything went still. Eerily, impossibly still as the broken shards began to bleed. Thick, dark-red liquid oozed from the broken pieces, pooling on the ground at their feet. It smelled of rust and decay, and the liquid pulsed as if it had a heartbeat.

Amber staggered back, her hand shaking. A thin cut ran along her knuckles, but it didn't bleed, only the mirror bled.

"What the hell…?" Jake whispered, staring at the bleeding glass.

The carnival was alive. It was a living thing, bleeding before them. Amber wiped her hands on her jeans, trying to steady herself.

The bleeding shards began to ripple and shift, forming words in the puddle at their feet:

**KEEP GOING. YOU'RE ALMOST THERE.**

Jake swallowed hard. "What do you think it means by "There"?" He asked while making air quotes with his fingers.

Amber shook her head. "I think it means we're screwed man."

But there was no going back. The mirrors behind them shifted again, blocking the path they had come from. There was only one way to go. Forward, deeper into the maze.

They stepped over the bleeding shards and moved cautiously through the twisting corridors. The air grew colder with every step, and the reflections whispered louder, their voices overlapping in a chaotic cacophony.

At the center of the maze, they found a single mirror, taller and darker than the others, its surface smooth and black as obsidian. Jake's heart pounded in his chest. This mirror felt different, it felt important. It felt, alive.

Amber reached out cautiously, placing a hand against the glass. It was warm, pulsing beneath her palm like the heartbeat of something alive.

Suddenly, the black surface began to ripple, like water disturbed by a pebble. For a brief moment, Jake thought he saw Jimmy's face again, flickering just beneath the surface.

"Jimmy..." Jake whispered, reaching toward the glass. But before he could touch it, the mirror went still again, reflecting only their own pale faces. The walls around them began to close in, the mirrors shifting and bending, trapping them in a tightening spiral.

The reflections grinned as they pressed closer, their eyes gleaming with malice.

"We have to move!" Jake said, pulling Amber with him.

They sprinted through the narrowing maze, the reflections clawing at the glass as they ran. The whispers followed them, growing louder, more insistent, until they were almost deafening.

Just when it seemed like the maze would swallow them whole, they burst through the final mirror, out into the open air of the carnival.

# Chapter 4:

The music from the carousel drifted through the night air. A slow, winding melody, discordant and hypnotic. The lights on the ride flickered unevenly, casting long, crooked shadows that seemed to writhe across the ground. The horses were frozen mid-gallop, their faces stretched in expressions of agony, as if caught between motion and pain.

Dare stood at the edge of the ride. His heart thudded in his chest, the overwhelming need to prove his bravery pulling him toward the carousel, even as something deep inside screamed for him to run.

When Jake and Amber caught up to him, Dare turned to them with a shaky grin.

"This thing's gotta lead somewhere, right? Feels... important."

Amber stared at the horses, her skin pale beneath the flickering lights.

"Feels like a trap."

Jake squinted at the ride. The air around the carousel was thick. He could feel it, the carnival feeding off their fear, drinking it in with every second they stayed.

Dare swung his leg over one of the carousel horses and grabbed the pole. The gears groaned to life, and the ride began to spin, slow at first, then faster, the music warping as the world blurred into a swirl of lights.

"Dare, wait!" Jake shouted, but it was too late. The carousel picked up speed, pulling Dare deeper into its grip.

Dare clung to the pole, his knuckles white. The ride spun faster and faster, the painted horses around him blurring into grotesque shapes, their mouths twisted open in silent screams, their eyes rolling back into their skulls.

Each rotation drained a piece of him, pulling at his energy like a leech. He felt his limbs grow heavier, his breath shallower. The edges of his vision darkened, like ink seeping across a page.

When Dare glanced down at his hands, he saw wrinkles, deep lines carved into his skin, as if years had passed in mere seconds. His heart pounded in his chest, fear rising like bile in his throat.

"What the hell!" Dare whispered, trying to shake it off. But the ride kept spinning, the world warping into a nightmare.

Jake and Amber ran alongside the carousel, the lights flickering wildly, the music twisting into a haunting wail.

"We have to get him off!" Amber shouted, her voice barely audible over the deafening hum of the ride.

Jake sprinted to the nearest horse, grabbing the pole with one hand, Dare's shirt with the other. The metal burned under his fingers, searing his skin, but he didn't let go. With a sharp tug, he yanked Dare free, pulling him off the carousel and the ride groaned to a halt.

The lights on the carousel dimmed, and the music stuttered into silence. Dare collapsed onto the ground, gasping for air. His hair, once jet black, was now streaked with gray. His hands shook violently, and when he looked at Jake, there was fear in his eyes, the kind of fear that leaves scars.

"I... I thought I was gonna die in there," Dare whispered, his voice hoarse. Jake knelt beside him, gripping his friend's shoulder.

"You're okay now. We've got you."

Amber crouched down, her eyes wide with concern.

"That ride, this whole place, it's feeding off us. It's alive, Jake. It's not just messing with our heads. It's stealing from us."

Jake nodded grimly. They couldn't afford to let their guard down again. As Dare tried to catch his breath, something strange happened. One of the carousel horses, the one Dare had ridden, twitched. Its head jerked slightly to the side, as if it had just taken its first breath in years.

The three teens watched in horror as the horse's eyes blinked, glassy and vacant, and its mouth stretched open in a wide, silent scream. Amber stumbled back, her hand over her mouth.

"What the hell...?"

Jake felt cold dread crawl down his spine. The ride wasn't just feeding off Dare, it was keeping a piece of him, forever.

"We need to go," Jake whispered, pulling Dare to his feet. "This place is getting stronger. The longer we stay, the worse it's gonna get."

Amber helped Dare steady himself, though his legs still trembled. The gray streaks in his hair wouldn't go away. It was a reminder of how close he'd come to being lost forever.

They moved away from the carousel, but the air around them felt heavier now, as if the carnival itself was aware of their presence, watching their every step.

Ahead, way off in the distance, loomed the Big Top Tent. Its red and white stripes rippling like a heartbeat beneath the glow of the carnival lights.

"We need to get to that tent," Jake said, determination in his voice.

"That's where we'll find Jimmy. Don't ask me how I know, because I don't really know, I can just feel it. Jimmys there."

Amber gave him a wary glance.

"And what if the carnival doesn't let us leave?"

Jake clenched his jaw. "Then we make it."

They kept moving, the twisted sounds of the carousel fading into the background as they made their way deeper into the carnival. But the air was thick with unseen danger, and Jake knew, whatever was waiting for them in the Big Top Tent would be worse than anything they'd faced so far.

As they made their way toward the tent, they passed by a row of empty booths. The carnival seemed deserted now, the crowds having melted away into the shadows.

Just when Jake thought they might have a moment to catch their breath, Madame Vespera appeared from the darkness, her glassy eyes gleaming under the flickering lights.

"You've made it far," she whispered, her voice low and serpentine. "But the carnival isn't done with you yet."

Amber stepped forward, the look of defiance dominated her aura. "What do you want from us?"

Madame Vespera smiled, a slow, unsettling grin. "It's not what I want, my dear. It's what the carnival wants. And it always gets what it wants."

She gave them a small, mocking bow, then disappeared into the shadows once more, her laughter lingering in the air like the toll of a bell.

Jake felt a chill run down his spine. The carnival was alive, and it wasn't going to let them leave without a fight.

They pushed forward, the lights of the Big Top Tent glowing brighter in the distance with every step. The smell of cotton candy and rot filled the air, and the ground beneath their feet seemed to pulse in time with the music that drifted faintly from the tent.

Dare stumbled slightly, still weakened from the carousel. Amber caught him, steadying him with a firm grip.

"You good?" she asked quietly.

Dare gave her a weak smile. "Yeah... just feels like I left a piece of me back there."

Jake didn't say anything, but he felt it too, the sense that the carnival was slowly peeling them apart, one layer at a time.

As they reached the edge of the Tunnel of dreams, Riley stopped, the feeling growing inside him told him that this one, was meant for him.

# Chapter 5:

The entrance to the Tunnel of Dreams loomed before Riley like the maw of some ancient creature. Its archway dripping with vines, the sign above painted in cracked gold lettering. Beneath the words, a warning had been scrawled in black paint: "Desire and Regret, Hand in Hand. Only one rider per boat, or else."

Amber, Jake, and Dare stood at his side, the glow of the lights around them pulsing like a heartbeat. Riley wiped sweat from his brow. The humid night pressed against his skin, but the deeper fear was the cold knot growing in his chest. He knew this ride was meant for him. He could feel it.

"You don't have to go in alone," Jake said, clapping Riley on the back.

Riley smirked, trying to mask the tremor in his voice.

"Come on, man. It's just a boat ride, right?"

His attempt at bravado felt paper-thin, but before anyone could protest, he stepped forward and climbed into the small, black gondola waiting at the dock.

The boat rocked gently under his weight, as if eager to carry him away. Without needing a push, it drifted forward, slipping into the tunnel's dark throat.

As Riley floated into the darkness, the tunnel closed around him, swallowing the world outside. The air grew cold, and the water beneath the boat shimmered like glass. Lanterns flickered overhead, casting faint, dancing lights that revealed flashes of strange, haunting images along the walls, scenes from his past, frozen in time.

He saw his parents' silhouettes, standing at opposite ends of a darkened room. Their angry voices filled the tunnel in bursts, "You don't care about us! You don't care about anyone but yourself!" his father shouted, while his mother wept silently, her back turned.

The water rippled, and another scene appeared, a younger Riley, standing alone at recess, watching the other kids play with their parents. His hadn't come that day. No one seemed to even notice him.

Riley clenched the sides of the boat, his heart pounding. The images felt too sharp, too raw, like freshly reopened wounds. The boat drifted on, deeper into the dream.

The tunnel shifted, the walls warping into surreal shapes. Riley's happiest memories bled into his worst fears, one overlapping the other like a twisted collage.

He saw himself older, holding a shimmering trophy, the crowd cheering his name. But just as quickly, the image flickered. The trophy turned to ash, and the applause faded, replaced by whispers of disappointment.

In another vision, he stood on a stage, playing guitar to a packed audience, the spotlight on him, every chord perfect. But the spotlight grew brighter, hotter, until he was blinded, drowning in white light that burned away the crowd and left him standing alone in the dark.

The boat glided deeper into the tunnel, and the visions began to press harder, more personal. He saw his friends, Jake,

Amber, and Dare walking away without him. They faded into shadows, their laughter echoing in the distance.

Riley reached out toward them, his hand trembling.

"Wait! Don't leave me!"

But his hand passed through the vision like smoke. The tunnel whispered back, "They were never really with you to begin with."

At the end of the tunnel, the boat drifted toward a platform bathed in dim, golden light. Madame Vespera stood waiting, her black dress rippling like liquid shadow. Her glassy eyes reflected Riley's exhausted face.

"You've seen what could have been," she whispered, her voice smooth and soothing, like a lullaby.

"And what may yet come." She smiled, a small, knowing grin.

"You can stay here, you know, where the dream is yours to shape."

Riley stared at her, his chest tight with fear and longing. "Stay...?"

"Here, you could be anything. Anyone. No regrets, no disappointments. Just... dreams."

She reached out a pale hand. "All you need to do is let go."

Riley hesitated. The pull was intoxicating, the thought of escaping all his fears, never having to confront what lay outside the tunnel.

The weight of reality, the uncertainty of friendships, the fear of failure, the inevitable loss. They'll leave, they always leave. Everyone leaves... it could all melt away.

But then he thought of Jake. Jake, dragging Dare off the cursed carousel, determined to save Jimmy. Amber, with her fierce determination, hiding her own fears but never backing down. Dare, still shaken but standing. They didn't give up.

Riley closed his eyes, his breath steadying. "No."

Madame Vespera's smile faltered for the first time. Her eyes darkened.

"I choose them," Riley whispered, the words firm despite the fear clawing at him.

"I'd rather fail with them than stay here without them."

Vespera's hand slowly withdrew, her grin fading into something cold and dangerous. "So be it."

The boat jerked suddenly, the current pulling Riley backward, dragging him back through the tunnel, faster and faster, as if the dream itself was rejecting him.

The boat shot out of the tunnel's entrance, splashing violently against the dock. Riley stumbled onto the platform, gasping for air. His hands trembled, but his mind was clear for the first time since entering the carnival.

Amber and Jake rushed toward him, relief flashing across their faces.

"Riley! You're okay!" Amber exclaimed, pulling him into a quick hug.

Riley leaned on Jake, his legs weak but steady enough to stand.

"That, that ride..." His voice was shaky, but he forced a grin. "It wasn't exactly the Tunnel of Love."

Amber gave him a look that said, "You're such a goober," but there was warmth behind it.

Jake clapped him on the back. "Glad you made it, man. I thought I lost you broham."

Dare, still pale from his encounter with the carousel, gave Riley a weak thumbs-up. "You look like you've seen some stuff man."

"You have no idea my dude," Riley muttered, rubbing his face with both hands.

But the choice was behind him now. They were still together, and that was what mattered.

As they regrouped near the Ferris Wheel, the air around them grew heavier, colder. The carnival was growing restless. They could feel it in the way the ground seemed to pulse, as if the earth beneath their feet was alive and waiting.

The group set off toward the Big Top, their hearts heavy with fear but united in their resolve. The carnival's lights flickered erratically, and the distant sound of twisted calliope music hummed like a warning in the back of their minds.

# Chapter 6:

The Ferris wheel towered before them, an enormous skeletal structure against the night sky, its lights flickering like dying embers. Each rotation groaned, the sound like a deep, rusted moan that echoed through the carnival. From below, the wheel seemed to stretch endlessly upward, as if it would never stop rising.

Jake, Amber, Riley, and Dare stood at the base of the ride, looking up at the slowly spinning monstrosity. Cold air clung to them, colder than the summer night should have allowed. The smell of burnt sugar and ozone drifted past on the breeze, mixing with the unsettling aroma of metal and dust.

"This is a bad idea," Amber muttered, folding her arms. The flickering lights cast long shadows across her face, making her look older and more tired than she was. Jake ignored the growing knot in his stomach and stepped toward the ticket booth. The booth was empty except for a small slot with a guitar emblem where tickets could be fed.

"Guess we're ridin'," Jake muttered, pulling out his personalized ticket, the small guitar emblem printed on it seeming to shimmer in the dim light. The paper felt heavier in his hand now, as if it carried the weight of something unseen.

They each slipped their tickets into the slot, and the ferris wheel groaned to life, the door to one of the compartments sliding open with a sharp hiss. "You sure about this?" Riley asked, his voice tense. "No," Jake admitted, "but it seems like we have to follow the rides to find Jimmy, so let's just get it over with."

The group climbed into the cabin, the door closing behind them with an ominous click. The wheel jolted and began to rise, lifting them slowly into the night. The carnival lights stretched out below them, glowing faintly, distorted by the haze that clung to the air like smoke.

As the wheel climbed higher, the cabin grew eerily silent. No sound but the creak of the metal frame and the distant hum of carnival music. It was as if the world outside had vanished, leaving them suspended in a dream, or a nightmare.

The higher they rose, the more the cabin seemed to change. The air inside turned cold and damp, and the glass windows fogged over with every breath they took. Shadows twisted and coiled at the edges of the compartment, creeping closer as the wheel ascended. Amber shivered, wrapping her arms around herself. "Something's... wrong."

"Yeah," Riley muttered back, staring out the foggy window. "Something's definitely wrong."

Suddenly, the fog on the window cleared, and what they saw on the other side should have been impossible.

Jake leaned closer to the glass, his heart pounding. Through the window, he saw his little sister standing in their living room, her back turned to him. She looked older, as if years had passed without him.

"Annie?" Jake whispered, pressing his hand to the glass.

In the vision, Annie turned slowly, her eyes dull and lifeless, her face a mask of cold indifference. "You left me," she said, her voice flat, empty. "You forgot about me."

Jake's stomach twisted. "No, I didn't." he whispered, but Annie's face faded, replaced by the reflection of his own terrified expression.

Amber tensed beside him. Her reflection had changed too. The glass showed her with pale makeup, red smeared lips, and a ragged clown costume. Her mouth opened in a silent scream, the painted grin splitting her face in two.

"No," Amber whispered, stepping back from the window. "No, no, no..."

Dare's knuckles turned white as he gripped the edge of the seat. He saw himself on the other side of the glass, paralyzed, trapped in a hospital bed, unable to move. His own eyes stared back at him, wide with helplessness. His lips moved, but no sound came out.

Riley sat perfectly still, his eyes glued to the window. He saw something too, but he didn't say what it was. His jaw clenched tighter with each passing second, his fists trembling in his lap.

The visions pressed against the glass like living things, threatening to spill into the cabin and consume them whole. The Ferris wheel continued its slow, deliberate ascent, the cabin tilting as it reached the top. For a brief moment, the carnival spread out beneath them like a twisted map. Rides bending in impossible angles, booths flickering like distant stars.

Then, without warning, the wheel lurched violently, and the cabin dropped into a freefall. They screamed as the world blurred around them, the lights of the carnival streaking past like shooting stars.

But the fall stopped abruptly and they were back at the bottom of the wheel, as if they had never left. The ride began to climb again, trapping them in a loop, forcing them to face their fears over and over.

Jake gritted his teeth, his heart slamming against his ribcage. Each rotation brought the same visions, his sister turning away, her face full of cold disappointment. The pain was relentless, gnawing at his mind, wearing him down.

Amber curled into herself, whispering "It's not real" over and over, though the reflection in the window said otherwise.

Dare's breathing grew shallow, his eyes wide with terror, trapped in the nightmare of his helplessness. Riley sat rigid, his knuckles white, his jaw locked. He refused to look at the window anymore.

"We can't stay on this thing," Jake muttered through clenched teeth. "It's trying to break us."

Jake scanned the cabin, his mind racing. There had to be a way off the ride, a way to stop it. His gaze landed on the emergency release lever near the door.

"Amber," Jake whispered, nudging her. "Help me with this."

Amber wiped her eyes, nodding shakily. Together, they gripped the lever and pulled with all their strength. The metal groaned, resisting at first, but then it gave way with a loud snap.

The cabin jolted, the door swinging open mid-ascent. Cold air rushed in, and the carnival lights flickered wildly below them.

"Go!" Jake shouted, his voice hoarse. "We jump on three!"

Without waiting for agreement, he counted down.

"One, two, three!"—and they leapt from the cabin just as it tilted toward the ground.

They hit the dirt with a heavy thud, rolling to a stop at the base of the wheel. The ground felt solid beneath them, and the lights on the Ferris wheel flickered once, then dimmed entirely.

Panting, the group lay sprawled on the ground, gasping for breath. They were off, but the fear still clung to them, thick and suffocating.

As they staggered to their feet, Jake glanced toward the center of the carnival, where the Big Top Tent loomed, glowing brighter than ever. It pulsed with an unnatural light, calling them forward like a beacon, or a warning.

"We're close," Jake whispered. "He's in there. I can feel it deep down in my plums."

"Oh come on, don't start with the plum talk." Amber said as she brushed dirt from her jeans.

Dare swallowed hard, still pale, but his fear was laced with resolve. "Alright. Let's do this."

Riley remained silent, his jaw tight, his eyes shadowed. Whatever he had seen in the cabin had left its mark, but he didn't speak of it.

Together, they turned toward the Big Top Tent and began to walk, their footsteps heavy but determined. The Ferris wheel groaned behind them, its twisted metal frame fading into the darkness.

# Chapter 7:

The Big Top Tent stood before them, its red-and-white stripes rippling in the night air like living skin, as if the tent itself were breathing. The entrance flaps billowed outward, welcoming them in with a silent invitation. The lights above the tent glowed with an unsettling warmth, casting long, spindly shadows that curled along the ground.

Jake, Amber, Riley, and Dare exchanged uneasy glances. This was it, the heart of the carnival. If Jimmy was anywhere, it would be inside this tent.

"You ready?" Jake asked quietly, glancing at the others.

Amber gave a determined nod, though her eyes held a flicker of fear. Riley and Dare shifted uneasily but said nothing. Whatever waited inside, they had come too far to turn back now.

"Let's do this," Jake whispered, pulling back the flap of the tent.

Inside, the air was thick and humid, filled with the cloying scents of cotton candy, sweat, and something rancid, like old meat left to spoil in the sun. A flickering spotlight illuminated the center of the tent, where a small stage had been erected. The seats surrounding it were filled with shadowy figures, unmoving, their faces hidden beneath cloaks and masks.

The four teens stood frozen at the entrance, the weight of unseen eyes pressing down on them. A low hum vibrated through the air, a strange, rhythmic pulse that thrummed in their bones. Then the spotlight shifted, and Mr. Grin stepped onto the stage.

Mr. Grin wore a black tailcoat and a wide-brimmed hat, his pale face stretched into an impossibly wide smile. His grin never faltered, never blinked, and it stretched too far, splitting his face at the seams. His teeth gleamed like polished bone under the light, and with each step he took, his presence seemed to pull the air tighter around them, like a noose slowly constricting.

"Ladies and gentlemen, boys and girls," Mr. Grin called, his voice a slick, oily whisper that slithered through the air.

"Welcome to the Midnight Show." With a dramatic flourish, he gestured to the stage, and there, at the center, stood Jimmy.

Jimmy's face was pale, his body rigid, frozen in place like a mannequin propped up on display. His eyes were wide with terror, his lips slightly parted as if he were about to scream, but no scream ever came. His fear was palpable, radiating off him in waves that seemed to feed the shadows lurking in the tent.

"Your friend has been very helpful," Mr. Grin whispered, circling Jimmy like a predator toying with its prey.

"He's been with us for some time now... helping us grow stronger." Jake's yelled out. "Let him go."

Mr. Grin's grin widened, impossibly, grotesquely. "Oh, I could let him go... but then, where would the fun be in that?"

He turned slowly, his empty eyes locking onto the group. "You see, it's not just Jimmy we came to see. It's all of you, and you'll stay with me."

The shadows around the tent began to shift, taking form, faces and limbs twisting into grotesque shapes, pale hands reaching toward the teens from the darkness. The air buzzed with whispered voices, promises, temptations, and threats, weaving a web of fear around them.

Mr. Grin spread his arms wide. "The carnival feeds on fear, you see... and your friend here, he looks delicious to me."

He tapped Jimmy's shoulder with a clawed finger. "But you? You look even tastier."

Jimmy's frozen form shuddered slightly, his lips trembling as if trying to speak, but Mr. Grin tightened his grip, and Jimmy went still again, his terror feeding the darkness around him.

Jake stepped forward, his heart racing, but his voice steady. "We're not afraid of you or this place."

Mr. Grin's smile faltered, just for a moment. The shadows around the tent hissed angrily, curling tighter like serpents.

"No?" Mr. Grin whispered, tilting his head. "Then why are you trembling?"

Jake swallowed hard. The truth was, he was terrified, but he was determined to not let it show. He wouldn't give Mr. Grin the satisfaction.

"We're taking Jimmy," Jake said, his voice low but firm. "And we're leaving."

Mr. Grin chuckled, a dry, hollow sound. "Oh, you think it's that simple?"

Suddenly, the tent shifted, and the stage morphed beneath their feet. The walls twisted, and the shadows leapt forward, dragging the teens into a nightmare world of their own making.

Jake found himself standing in his sister's room, but Annie was gone. The walls were lined with mirrors, each one reflecting a different version of himself, every failure, every moment he had let someone down.

Amber stood in a room filled with balloons, each one bursting with laughter, mocking, shrill, and endless. The walls closed in on her, and when she looked down, her hands were covered in white paint and greasepaint streaked down her face.

Dare lay trapped in a hospital bed, his limbs bound, unable to move. Doctors and nurses moved around him, but no one looked at him, no one heard him, no one cared.

Riley stood alone on a stage, bathed in light, but there was no one in the audience, just rows of empty seats. The silence was deafening, and no matter how hard he tried to speak, no sound came out.

Jake stood firm, breathing hard. The mirrors surrounded him, closing in, but then he remembered what mattered.

His sister. Annie needed him. She still needed him, and he promised to never leave her alone and to always be there when she needed him. And he wouldn't let the carnival take that from him or her.

With a cry, Jake slammed his fist into the nearest mirror, shattering it. The pieces fell away like dust, and the room dissolved around him.

They all stared into the empty void of the mirror and froze. They watched in horror as the real carnival stretched out before them.

The Ferris wheel groaned as it turned, made of screaming torsos and writhing limbs. Faces pressed against the surface, mouths open in silent agony. The lights on the wheel blinked, pulsing like beating hearts strung together in place of bulbs.

The carousel twisted slowly, its horses sculpted from disjointed arms and legs stitched together with red thread. The floor beneath it churned with bloody ribbons that snaked across the ground.

Stalls and booths along the walls were piled with severed hands, some twitching as if still alive. The hands held out prizes, their fingers stiff and lifeless, offering empty promises in hushed, dead voices. "Play with us," they whispered. "Please... play."

Jake felt bile rise in his throat. Every ride, every machine, every booth was made from the lost children, the ones who had vanished into the carnival over the years, now fused into its living nightmare.

"They're trapped," Amber whispered, horror dawning in her voice. "This place... it's holding them."

Then the mirrors void began to shift again, showing visions of what might become of them.

Jake saw his sister, Annie, stretched along the tent walls, her body twisted and pinned like an insect, calling out to him in a faint, distant voice. "You promised Jake."

Amber saw herself transformed into a grotesque clown, her smile carved into her face, forever laughing.

Riley saw himself stuck on the Ferris wheel, spinning endlessly, his voice lost in the roar of screams.

Dare saw his body trapped beneath the carousel, his friends walking away without ever noticing him.

The mirror's images grew more frantic, each vision more horrifying than the last. The future twisted and warped, showing them the terrible price of failure.

"We need to get out of here," Dare muttered, his voice barely audible. "Now."

Suddenly, the mirrors void bulged outward, as though something inside was trying to escape. Fingers pressed against the glass, followed by a face that stretched too wide, ***Mr. Grin***.

His grin widened beyond what should have been possible. "You belong to us," he whispered, his voice a horrible symphony of children's screams. "You will be part of us."

The mirror shattered violently, sending shards flying through the air. Each shard bled, and the cuts they left felt like memories that belonged to the lost children being forced into their minds.

Jake began breaking every mirror he could see. Amber, Riley, and Dare did the same, confronting their fears head-on, refusing to let them define them. The illusions shattered, one by one, until the four of them stood together again in the center of the tent.

Mr. Grin stood back at the edge of the stage, his grin faltering for the first time. "Stop this foolishness now you little brats."

Jake stepped forward, his eyes blazing with determination. "We're not afraid of you."

The tent groaned, the walls trembling as the carnival's power began to wane. The shadows hissed and writhed, but they couldn't touch the teens now.

Together, they grabbed Jimmy's frozen form, pulling him away from Mr. Grin.

Mr. Grin snarled, his grin warping into something hideous. "You can't escape! The carnival never lets anyone go, the only way to possibly leave is in pieces!"

But it was too late. The magic holding the carnival together was unraveling. The walls of the tent began to collapse, folding inward like fabric caught in a windstorm. The shadows screamed, twisting and writhing as the light consumed them. The ground shook violently, and the rides outside began to topple, crumbling into dust.

"RUN!" Jake shouted, dragging Jimmy toward the exit. The group sprinted toward the open flap of the tent, the ground crumbling beneath their feet. Behind them, Mr. Grin's voice echoed, distorted, furious, and fading. "Until we meet again children!"

They burst out of the tent just as it collapsed in on itself, the walls folding into nothingness. The carnival lights flickered one last time before going dark, and the night fell silent. They stood in the empty field, the cool night breeze brushing against their faces. The carnival was gone, only a vacant lot remained.

Jake turned to Jimmy, who was pale and shaking, but alive. "You okay, man?"

Jimmy nodded slowly, though his hands still trembled. "Yeah... I think so."

Amber wrapped her arm around Jimmy's shoulder. "Let's get out of here."

Together, the group made their way back toward town, the distant stars glimmering above them.

But even as they walked, Jake couldn't shake the feeling that something was still watching them, something waiting. And in the distance, a faint strain of carnival music drifted on the breeze.

# Chapter 8:

The field around them was silent, the carnival gone without a trace, but the air still hummed with a strange tension, like the moment right before a thunderstorm hits. The group stumbled through the tall grass, the glow of the Big Top Tent now a ghostly afterimage burned into their vision.

Jake held onto Jimmy, whose steps were unsteady. His face was pale, his dark eyes distant, as if a part of him was still lost inside the carnival's web.

Amber glanced over her shoulder toward the empty space where the carnival had been. "It doesn't feel like it's really over," she whispered.

Jake nodded grimly. "We need to finish it, for good. Let's find that deranged puppet."

Madame Vespera's cryptic words echoed in Jake's mind: "The carnival always gets what it wants."

But maybe there was a way to break its hold. Maybe if they destroyed the enchanted puppet at the gate, the one who had given them the tickets and started this whole mess to begin with.

Riley ran a hand through his hair, still rattled. "If the carnival's gone, how do we get back to the puppet?"

Dare, still pale from his carousel ordeal, shifted uneasily. "What if destroying the puppet brings the carnival back?"

"It doesn't matter," Jake said, his voice steady. "If we don't break the connection, it'll follow us forever."

Amber locked eyes with Jake. "So, we go back."

Jake nodded. "We go back."

The group retraced their steps toward the edge of the field, where the flickering lights of the old ticket booth had first drawn them into the carnival. They pushed through the tall grass and weeds, the night air growing colder as they moved.

When they reached the spot where the booth had stood, the puppet was still there, slumped inside the cracked glass, its lifeless eyes staring blankly ahead.

"That thing gave us the tickets," Dare whispered, his voice hoarse. "That's the connection. It's how we got in."

Amber shivered. "We have to destroy it. Now."

Jake reached into his jacket pocket and pulled out the ticket stubs they had kept. They glowed faintly, their edges curling as if they knew their time was up.

"We need something to break it," Jake said, glancing around. "Something sharp."

Riley pulled a rusted crowbar from the weeds nearby, tossing it to Jake. "This should do it."

Jake gripped the crowbar tightly, his heart hammering in his chest. He took a deep breath and stepped toward the booth. As he raised the crowbar, the puppet's glassy eyes flicked upward, locking onto Jake.

"Don't do this," the puppet whispered, its voice a rasping hiss. "It won't end well for you if you do."

Jake hesitated for a moment, but then Amber's hand rested on his shoulder. "Do it," she whispered. "Before it pulls us back."

With a sharp cry, Jake swung the crowbar down. The glass shattered, sending shards flying in all directions. The puppet's head snapped to the side, and a low, guttural groan echoed from deep within its chest as the gears inside it ground to a halt.

The carnival lights flickered in Jake's mind, like an old film reel catching fire, and then everything went dark. The air shifted, and a heavy silence fell over the field.

For a moment, nothing happened. Then the ground beneath their feet began to tremble. The wind howled, and the sky above them seemed to ripple, as if reality itself was coming undone.

"Is it coming back," Riley asked, gripping the edge of the broken booth for balance.

Jake dropped the crowbar and grabbed Jimmy's arm. "We should probably go now."

The group sprinted through the field, their feet pounding against the earth as the world behind them began to collapse. The sound of calliope music twisted and warped, growing louder, more frantic, as the carnival fought to keep its grip on their reality.

The air smelled of ozone and burning sugar, and the distant laughter of Mr. Grin echoed through the night, growing fainter with each step they took.

They reached the edge of the field just as the last remnants of the carnival dissolved into the night. The music faded, the laughter silenced, and the wind died down, leaving only the soft hum of crickets in the distance.

They collapsed onto the grass, panting, their hearts racing. The ticket stubs in Jake's pocket disintegrated into ash, blown away by the breeze.

"I think it's finally over," Amber whispered, though her voice held no relief, only exhaustion.

Jimmy sat beside her, his eyes wide and haunted. "I thought I'd be stuck there forever," he murmured. "I could feel it pulling me deeper."

Jake gave him a reassuring nod. "You're safe now bro. We weren't about to leave you there, no matter what."

They sat in silence for a long time, watching the stars above them. The night was still, peaceful, but the weight of what they had endured hung over them like a shadow.

Dare ran a hand through his streaked gray hair. "So... what now?"

Riley forced a grin, though it didn't quite reach his eyes. "I say we never go near a carnival again."

Amber chuckled softly, nudging Riley with her elbow. "Agreed."

Jake smiled faintly, but his gaze lingered on the empty field. The carnival was gone, but the memory of it would stay with them forever. Just as they began to rise, Jake heard something faint on the wind, a distant strain of carnival music, so quiet it could have been a trick of his imagination.

He glanced toward the empty lot, his heart skipping a beat. But there was nothing there, only shadows and grass, swaying gently in the breeze.

"We should go now guys, I can feel it deep down in my pluuuums," Jake said with that goofy sound in his voice.

"Don't start that again!" Amber interjected loudly half grinning as she shoved him.

The group began the long walk back to town, the night air cool and crisp around them. The ordeal was behind them, but the bond they shared was stronger now, forged in fear, tested by the nightmare they had survived.

They didn't know what lay ahead, but whatever it was, they would face it together.

And as they disappeared into the night, Mr. Grin's whispered promise lingered: "Until we meet **again.**"

# Chapter 9:

The next morning, the sun rose over the quiet streets of town, casting long golden rays across the empty sidewalks. Birds chirped in the trees, and the world carried on as if nothing had happened, as if the carnival had never been there at all.

Jake sat on the curb outside Sandy's Diner, the cool morning breeze brushing his face. His jacket, scuffed and torn from the night's events, still clung to him like a second skin. The smell of bacon and coffee drifted from the diner doors, comforting but oddly distant, like a dream he wasn't fully awake from yet.

Amber, Riley, and Dare sat beside him, each lost in their own thoughts. Jimmy leaned against the wall, sipping from a glass of water, his eyes downcast and hollow. He hadn't said much since they'd left the field, as if words were too fragile to contain what he'd been through.

The waitress brought over four milkshakes, setting them down with a tired smile.

"Rough night?" she asked, her voice light but curious.

Jake gave a small nod. "You could say that."

The group sat in silence for a while, the milkshakes slowly melting in the morning heat. The world outside seemed too normal, too bright, after the nightmare they had just survived. Every clink of a spoon or scrape of a chair felt surreal, like the real world had become just as strange as the carnival.

Finally, Amber broke the silence, stirring her milkshake with a long, slow motion.

"So... what the hell just happened?"

Dare gave a weak chuckle, rubbing the gray streak in his hair. "We kicked some butt, that's what happened."

Riley shook his head, running his thumb along the rim of his glass. "Barely." His eyes were shadowed, his usual jokes gone. The carnival had taken more from him than he was willing to admit.

Jake glanced toward Jimmy, who sat quietly, tracing invisible patterns on the table with his finger. "You good, Jimmy?"

Jimmy hesitated, then gave a small nod. "I... I think so. But it's weird. I remember everything, and nothing, all at once."

He shook his head, his voice barely a whisper. "It felt like I was gone for years."

Jake nodded thoughtfully. "It's over now man," he said, trying to convince himself as much as the others.

"We're done with it and all other carnivals from here on out."

Amber glanced out the diner window toward the empty lot where the carnival had stood. The field was quiet now, but the memory of it lingered like a bruise, painful, impossible to ignore.

"They'll never believe us, will they?" she asked softly.

"Heck no bro. No one will." Riley gave a hollow laugh. "I barely believe it myself."

Dare shifted uncomfortably in his seat. "I keep thinking about that puppet. What if destroying it wasn't enough? What if."

"Don't," Jake interrupted, his voice sharp. "It's done. We destroyed the puppet. We broke the connection."

Amber nodded, though she didn't look convinced. None of them were.

As they finished their milkshakes, Jake noticed something on the bulletin board near the door, a flyer pinned beneath a thumbtack. It was faded, as if it had been there for years, but the image was unmistakable: **COMING SOON—THE CARNIVAL RETURNS.**

Jake's blood ran cold. He stared at the flyer, his heart pounding in his chest.

"Dudes..." Jake whispered, pointing toward the board.

The others turned to look. Amber's breath caught in her throat, Riley choked on his drink, and Dare just stared, his hands gripping the edge of the table. The carnival's logo was the same. The colors were the same. And at the bottom, written in bold red letters, was the words: **COMING THIS FALL.**

Jake tore the flyer off the board, crumpling it in his hand. "No," he whispered fiercely. "No way."

Outside the diner, the world continued on as if nothing had changed. People walked their dogs, kids rode bikes down the street, and the distant sound of church bells rang out, calm and familiar.

But the group knew better. The carnival wasn't gone. Not really. Riley leaned back in his seat, exhaling slowly. "If it comes back..." His voice trailed off, but the weight of the unspoken words hung heavy in the air.

Jake unfolded the crumpled flyer in his hand and stared at it one last time.

"If it comes back, we'll be ready."

Amber gave him a small, determined smile. "Yeah. I guess we will."

Dare ran a hand through his hair, shaking his head with a nervous laugh. "Are we seriously gonna do this again?"

Jake nodded, tucking the flyer into his pocket. "If we have to."

Jimmy looked up from his empty glass, his voice quiet but firm. "We'll stick together this time. No one gets left behind."

The group exchanged a solemn look, and for the first time since the carnival had vanished, Jake felt a flicker of hope. They had survived the nightmare once. They could do it again, and possibly destroy it so no more kids get taken, maybe even release the souls of the ones already imprisoned there.

As they stepped out of the diner into the bright morning light, the sound of the door chime seemed to linger in the air longer than it should have, like the faint echo of carnival music, just on the edge of hearing.

Jake paused, glancing back toward the empty field one last time. The wind rustled through the tall grass, and for a brief moment, he thought he saw the flicker of neon lights, just beyond the trees. But when he blinked, the lights were gone, and the field was empty once more.

Amber nudged him gently. "You okay?" Jake forced a smile. "Yeah, just had a feeling in my pl-."

"Yeah, yeah, in your plums. Now shush it Mr." Amber said, cutting him off before he could finish.

They walked down the quiet street together, the morning stretching out before them, full of possibilities. But in the back of Jake's mind, the carnival's music still played, soft, distant, and waiting.

They didn't know what the future held. But whatever came next, they would face it together. And if the carnival ever returned, they would be ready.

As they disappeared down the street, the morning sunlight glinted off the crumpled flyer in hanging halfway out of Jake's pocket, casting a faint, eerie glow.

And somewhere, in the shadows between worlds, **Mr. Grin smiled.**

**Next books in the series:**
**Neon Dreams**

When reality glitches, where do you run?

Ty and his friends thought they were just spending another weekend geeking out over Dungeons & Dragons—until the séance. Now, they're trapped in a neon-lit dreamscape where monsters from their campaigns roam the streets and every choice could mean life or eternal sleep.

The only way out? They'll have to rely on their wits, friendships, and the same skills they use around the gaming table to survive. But there's a catch—the deeper they venture, the more twisted and surreal the world becomes. Shadows of their worst fears haunt every corner, and a sinister force known as *The Architect* is playing a game of its own, waiting to claim their souls.

The clock is ticking. Will Ty and his friends escape before the dream consumes them... or will they be stuck in *Neon Dreams* forever?

**"An 80s nostalgia-drenched thrill ride**

### *Satanic Panic: The Midnight Gospel*

It's 1989, and the sleepy town of Ashwood is gripped by fear. Kids are missing, strange symbols are appearing on doors, and parents are pointing fingers at everything from heavy metal to Dungeons & Dragons. The airwaves are full of preachers and politicians screaming about Satanic cults lurking behind every corner. But for B, Crystal, Heather, Mike, and Sam, this is more than just another wild conspiracy—it's all terrifyingly real.

When the five friends stumble onto an ancient, underground cult known as The Midnight Gospel, they realize the danger is far worse than anything on the nightly news. The cult isn't just spreading fear—it's planning a ritual to summon something far more evil than anyone could imagine: Belial, a demon from the depths of the abyss.

Now, with the next full moon fast approaching, the kids must infiltrate the cult's hidden lair, face down shadowy horrors, and stop the ritual before the darkness consumes their town—and their souls.

But evil never fights fair, and the closer they get to the truth, the harder it becomes to tell what's real and what's a nightmare. With every step, the shadows grow deeper. And if they make one mistake... Belial will escape.

Part 80s nostalgia, part occult thriller, and all heart-pounding horror, *Satanic Panic: The Midnight Gospel* is a pulse-pounding ride through the hysteria of a paranoid decade—where friendship, fear, and fate collide.

### *Skin of the Moon*

Beneath the blood-red moon, the curse awakens.

In the remote desert town of Black Hollow, Arizona, something ancient stirs. People are vanishing, and the ones who return... aren't the same. Their skin peels away to reveal fur, teeth sharpen into fangs, and yellow eyes burn with hunger.

When Jesse, Dana, Ty and Holly encounter the creature responsible, a cursed Skinwalker trapped between human and beast, their lives spiral into a nightmare they can't escape. As the curse spreads, warping animals and townsfolk alike, they race to uncover the truth buried deep in the desert.

But the curse doesn't just twist bodies, it consumes souls.

With Holly already showing signs of transformation and the full moon rising, Jesse must decide how far he's willing to go to save his friends. Time is running out, and the line between friend and predator is beginning to blur.

In Black Hollow, the only way to survive the night... is to feed. Some curses can't be broken, they can only be passed on.

# Also by B. Humphrey

**Bigfoot Vs**
Bigfoot Vs Werewolves
Bigfoot Vs Vampires
Bigfoot Vs Aliens
Bigfoot Vs Yeti
Bigfoot Vs Werebear
Bigfoot Vs Mothman
Bigfoot Vs The Kandahar Giant
Bigfoot Vs Chimera
Bigfoot Vs Loch Ness Monster
Bigfoot Vs Wendigo
The Great Cryptid Wars
The Moon Curse Saga
Bigfoot Vs: The Collector's Edition Books 1-10

**Retro Horrors: The Lost Decade**
Cassette Ghosts
Summer of the Black Star
The Arcade Incident

Dead End Drive – In
The Polaroid Project
Endless Paths: The Choose-Your-Own Doom Chronicles
Neon Dreams
The Forgotten Carnival
Satanic Panic
Skin of the Moon


**Sporefall**
Sporefall


**The Autumn Folklore Chronicles**
The Forest Of Forgotten Names
The Witch Of Windspindle Hollow
The Burrowfolk Chronicles


**The Fall Of America**
The Final Directive


**The Phantom Finders Club**
A Haunting On Maplewood Street
The Secrets Of Old Fort Tower
Ghosts OF The Infirmary

**The Saturn Outlaws**
The Saturn Outlaws: Sky-Bandits of the Void Frontier


**The Starling Sleuths**
Detective Starling vol. 1
Detective Starling Vol. 2


**Winter Horrors**
Whispers of the Wendigo
Cold Cuts
The Dark Beneath


**Standalone**
The Witch of Blackwood Hollow
The Storied Mind
The Great Cryptid Wars
Chronicles of the Hairy Kind: A Field Log by Thaddeus Grieve